Nana's Christmas SNOWFLAKES

Sue Gill Harris

WestBow Press books may be ordered through booksellers or by contacting:

WestBow Press
A Division of Thomas Nelson & Zondervan
1663 Liberty Drive
Bloomington, IN 47403
www.westbowpress.com
844-714-3454

llustrated by Rumar Yongco

ISBN: 978-1-6642-0872-8 (sc)
ISBN: 978-1-6642-0873-5 (e)

Library of Congress Control Number: 2020919969

Print information available on the last page.

WestBow Press rev. date: 11/10/2020

This book is dedicated to my grandchildren:
Andi, Rhett, Xander and Hayley
I love you to eternity and beyond
And so does God

Andi, Rhett, Xander and Hayley arrived at Nana's house on Christmas Eve. When they went inside, they found Nana sitting in her favorite chair working on one of her "projects."

"What are you doing with that white string?" asked Hayley, the youngest.

Andi, the oldest, replied, "That's not string; it's crochet thread."

"That's right," said Nana; "I'm working on Christmas snowflakes for each of you to hang on the tree. Sit down and I'll tell you all about it."

As the children sat down around Nana, she began to tell them about her Christmas snowflakes.

"I've always been told that snowflakes have 6 sides, and I have finally figured out why:

The first side is for

God, The Father, Maker of Everything!

The second side is for

Jesus, His Son and our Savior. Christmas is for celebrating His birth.

The third side is for

The Wise Men who followed the star that shone over Bethlehem and guided them to baby Jesus.

The fourth side is for

The Shepherds to whom an angel announced the birth of Christ on that very first Christmas.

The fifth side is for

You and Me (and all of mankind), whom Jesus came to teach and to save.

The Sixth side is for

The Holy Spirit, whom Jesus asked God to send to us - to dwell in our hearts.

The inside of the snowflake is the webbing that binds us all together. **AND**, if we believe in Jesus, we're washed as white as . . .

SNOW!

John 3:16 says: For God so loved the world that He gave his one and only Son, that whoever believes in Him shall not perish but have eternal life.

Now, here's one for each of you. Go hang them on the tree as a reminder that Christmas is not about elves and toys. It's about the birth of Jesus and the joy, love, and peace that He brings us. You can find reminders of Jesus in many, many things around you; all you have to do is look with your heart."

Nana's Christmas Snowflakes

How to Crochet Nana's Snowflake

I like to use Red Heart white Scrubby Sparkle 3oz yarn.

A size 3 crochet hook should make a 3 inch snowflake; size 4 should make a 4 inch snowflake.

Ch6, slst to form a circle

R1: ch 3 (counts as a dc), 2dc, ch2, *(3dc, ch2) repeat 4 more times (you should have 6 groups of 3dc separated by ch2) slst in top of beginning ch3

R2: slst to first ch2 space, ch3, 2dc, ch2, 3dc, *(3dc, ch2, 3dc) in each ch2 space, slst into top of beg ch3

R3: same as R2, but between each (3dc, ch2, 3dc) add 1dc into space between each (3dc, ch2, 3dc) below

Finish off by making a large loop for hanging and tie off.

About the Author

Sue Gill Harris is a child of God, a wife, a mother, a grandmother, and a retired (after 42 years) elementary teacher. She enjoys being creative through various hobbies including writing, crocheting, knitting, and sewing. She is also active in her church as a Sunday School teacher and VBS director/teacher.

Printed in the United States
By Bookmasters